To all of our family and friends!
Thank you for your love and support!

Constance the Cowlet

Illustration © 2019 Andrew Lofton
www.andrew-and-friends.com

Constance was born
in a sunny pasture, on a big farm.

Her mother, Cornelia the Cow, was delighted!
Her father, Buster the Bull, was so proud!

The little family was very happy on the farm.
They had green grass to eat, swishy water to drink,
and shady trees to relax under during hot afternoons.

As soon as Constance could stand,
she wobbled away to explore the green pasture.
There were many friends on the farm.

First, she met some baby ducklings by the pond.
She liked how they waddled.

Next, she met a horse named Patches.
She liked the warm whinny sound that he made
as he greeted her.

Finally she met Pansy the Pig.

"Meet my piglets," said their mother.

"What are piglets?" asked Constance.
"Why, they are baby pigs," said Pansy.

"You are a baby cow, so you must be a cowlet,"
oinked Pansy, with a great deal of authority.

Constance liked how they wallowed
in the green grass and messy mud.

Constance bid the piglets a good day and waddled away like the ducklings, whinnied like her friend Patches, while taking an occasional wallow on the cool, green grass of the pasture.

She kept repeating,
"Constance the Cowlet" to herself. She liked how it made her sound important.

Constance was crowded into a big pen with some other much larger cows. She heard a cowboy say, "off to the SALE BARN," as he slammed the gate.

Then they started to move.

They rolled away from the big farm and up the hill. Constance didn't know what a sale barn was, but she didn't think she was going to like it.

Constance was frightened.

Dinner time came and Cornelia the Cow and
Buster the Bull began to worry when Constance
did not return from her walk.
They looked for their daughter everywhere!

They asked the ducklings. They asked Patches.
They asked Pansy. No one had seen her for hours!

Suddenly, Buster remembered seeing the cattle trailer rolling up the hill. He had been on that trailer before when he was brought to the big farm!

Buster fretted and feared and Cornelia wondered and worried. Buster mooed a most woeful moo. Cornelia mooed her most woeful moo, too.

The cows were so loud that Phil the Dairy Farmer
came out to see what all the mooing was about.
He saw Buster. He saw Cornelia. But he did not see Constance.

Meanwhile, Constance was led into the
sale barn; she was very afraid. There was no
green grass, no shady trees, and no swishy
water. There were only falling fences and rusty
gates. She missed her mom and dad. She was
also very hungry.

Then Constance heard a strange voice and numbing numbers, "250 do I hear 275, 275 do I hear 300 for this fine animal? She's as good as can be, folks, 300, do I hear 325? 325!"

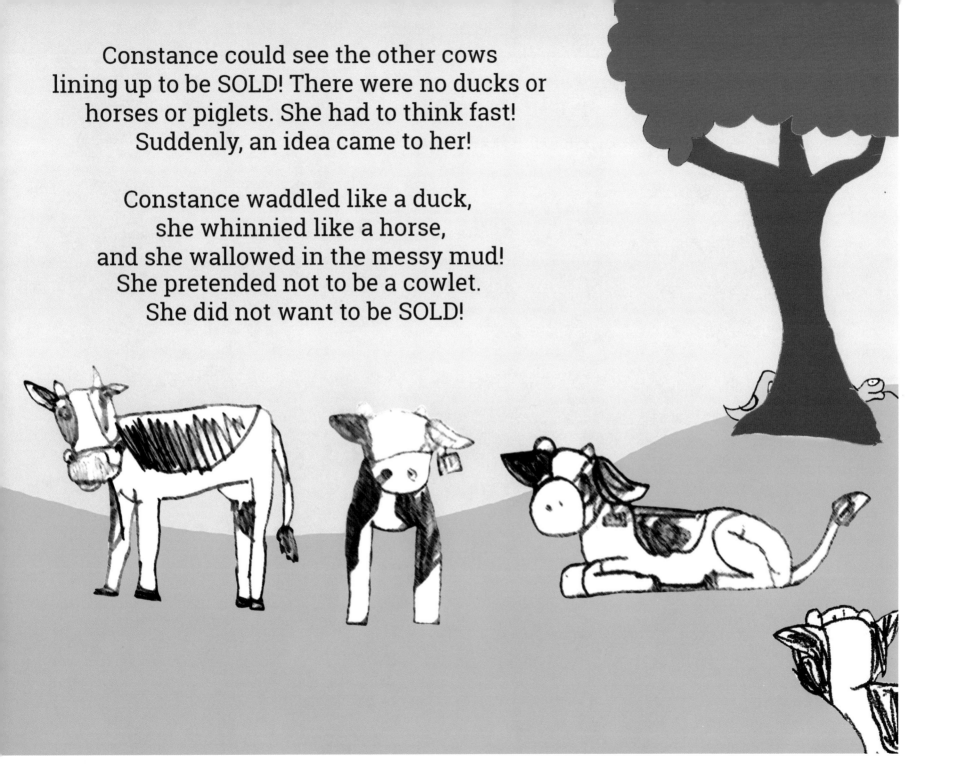

Constance could see the other cows
lining up to be SOLD! There were no ducks or
horses or piglets. She had to think fast!
Suddenly, an idea came to her!

Constance waddled like a duck,
she whinnied like a horse,
and she wallowed in the messy mud!
She pretended not to be a cowlet.
She did not want to be SOLD!

Constance heard someone speaking to her.
"What are you doing here, little one? You don't
belong here.You are much too small for
the sale barn."

It was a little girl who introduced herself as Megan.
She was wearing overalls and a baseball cap.
She had curly hair and glasses.

Of all the friends Constance met that day, Megan was her favorite! She liked how Megan kissed her on the nose and scratched her ears.

Megan took charge of things and told an adult about Constance.

The next thing she knew, Megan was holding tightly to Constance as they rode together in the back of a pickup truck.

Constance began to recognize the big farm.
She heard her mom, Cornelia the Cow, and her dad,
Buster the Bull, mooing very loudly.
She saw the farmer waving his hands wildly
and pointing to the fence.

All at once, Constance was back with her parents!
They were overjoyed to see their baby calf again.
"How did you escape the Sale Barn?" Cornelia asked.

"I waddled like a duck. I whinnied like a horse and
wallowed in the messy mud. I was afraid. I didn't
want anyone to know that I am a cowlet."

"A cowlet?" laughed her mother.

"Pansy the Pig called me a cowlet," remarked Constance. Cornelia rolled her eyes heavenward and mooed a sighing kind of moo.

"Constance, you are a calf, my brave girl -- a baby cow and you are never to wander so far away again!" said Cornelia.

Buster the bull grinned, "A clever and brave little cowlet you are!" he said.

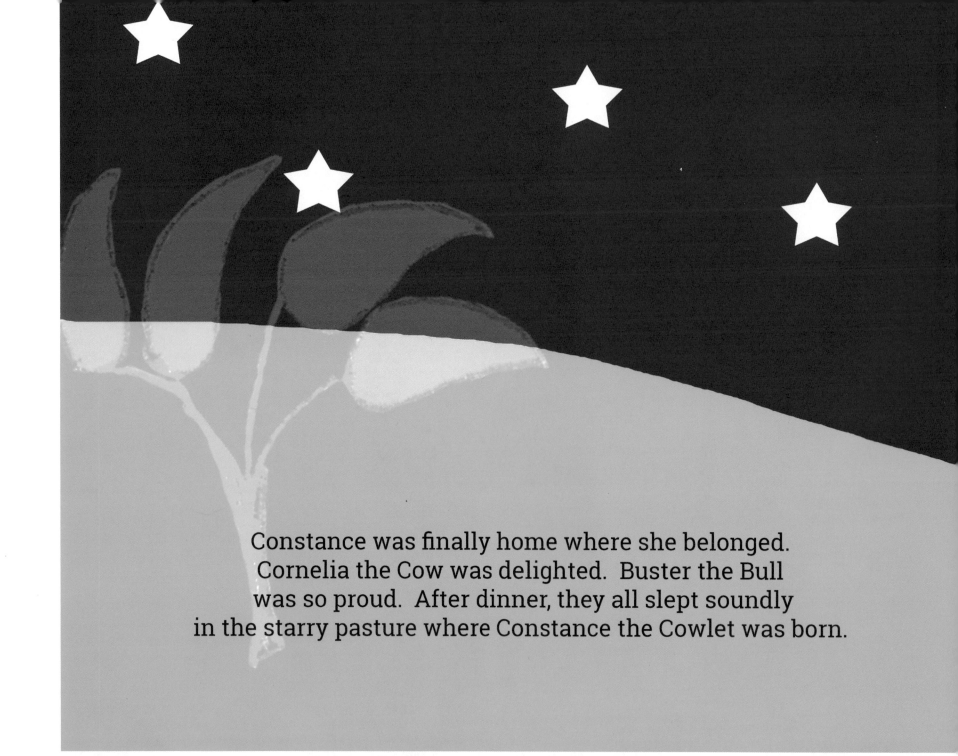

Constance was finally home where she belonged.
Cornelia the Cow was delighted. Buster the Bull
was so proud. After dinner, they all slept soundly
in the starry pasture where Constance the Cowlet was born.

CPSIA information can be obtained at www.ICGtesting.com
Printed in the USA
LVIW010010201020
669243LV00009B/48